I   Graves, Sue
GRA   Hippo owns up

DATE DUE			
JAN 3 1 2018	NO 1 8 ON		
7 2018	NO 2 7 19		
FEB 7 1 2018			
MAR 0 3 2018			
MAY 1 8 2018			

HiPPO OWNS UP

WRITTEN BY SUE GRAVES

ILLUSTRATED BY TREVOR DUNTON

WINDMILL BOOKS

Published in 2017 by **Windmill Books**, an Imprint of Rosen Publishing
29 East 21ˢᵗ Street, New York, NY 10010

Series Editor: Jackie Hamley
Series Designer: Cathryn Gilbert

Cataloging-in-Publication Data

Names: Graves, Sue. | Dunton, Trevor, illustrator.
Title: Hippo owns up / by Sue Graves; illustrated by Trevor Dunton.
Description: New York : Windmill Books, 2016. | Series: Behavior matters | Includes
index, table of contents, and glossary.
Identifiers: ISBN 9781499480894 (pbk.) | ISBN 9781499480818 (library bound)
| ISBN 9781499480740 (6 pack)
Subjects: LCSH: Honesty–Juvenile fiction. | Truthfulness and falsehood–Juvenile fiction.
Classification: LCC PZ7.G7754 Hi 2016 | DDC [F]–dc23

Manufactured in the United States of America
CPSIA Compliance Information: Batch #BS16PK: For Further Information contact Rosen Publishing, New York, New York at 1-800-237-9932.

CONTENTS

It was Tuesday and Hippo was having a **bad day**. He had gotten up late.

He had **missed breakfast**.

He was **late** for school, too.
Miss Bird was not happy with him.

4

Then Miss Bird gave him lots of math to do.
But Hippo was **too hungry** to do it.

Page 6
Questions
1 – 22

21 × 3
= 0 + 8
50
~~100~~

4 + 2

5

Hippo looked at the clock. It was nearly lunchtime. Mrs. Croc always made chocolate cake for lunch on Tuesdays. She always put lots of chocolate icing on the top, too.

Hippo thought about the chocolate cake and the chocolate icing. His tummy **rumbled loudly**. Everyone heard. Everyone giggled. Miss Bird told them to **get on with their work**.

Menu...
Tuesday
Soup
+
chocolate
cake

But the more Hippo thought about the
chocolate cake, the louder his tummy rumbled.
Then he got the **hiccups**! The hiccups were
very, very loud.

Everyone laughed. Miss Bird got mad.
She said Hippo was **disturbing everyone**.
She told him to go to the kitchen to get a
drink of water.

9

Hippo went to the kitchen. The big chocolate cake was on the table. He went to get a closer look. It looked **delicious**. It smelled **delicious**. He decided to try a tiny bit of it. He picked up a spoon and took a bit of cake. **It tasted wonderful!**

Hippo stared at the cake. Now there was a little hole on one side of the cake. He tried to smooth the icing over the hole. But it looked worse. He took some cake from the other side to try to even it up. But it looked **worse** than before.

Hippo was **worried**. He wanted to make the cake look better. He took more and more cake. It tasted delicious, but the more he took, the worse it looked. Soon there was **no cake** left at all!

Hippo went back to class. Miss Bird said he had
been gone a **long time**. She told him to **get going**
with his math.

But Hippo could not get on with his math.
His tummy felt too full and he felt too sick.
He **felt bad** for eating all the cake.

Just then the bell rang for lunchtime. Everyone lined up. But Mrs. Croc had some bad news. She said there was no chocolate cake because it was **all gone**. She said Hattie, the school cat, must have eaten it. She said Hattie was a bad cat. Hippo said **nothing**.

Everyone ate their lunch, but Hippo was **not hungry**. He was not hungry at all. Mrs. Croc was worried.

Hippo was **always** hungry and he always ate his lunch. She thought he must be **ill**. She sent him to Miss Bird.

Hippo told Miss Bird about the chocolate cake. He told her that he had eaten it, not Hattie. Miss Bird said that he should **not** have eaten the cake but that he was brave **to own up**. She said he should think about how to **make things right**.

Hippo thought really hard. He told Miss Bird he had to **say sorry** to everyone for eating the cake. He said he had a **good idea** to make things right, too. He told Miss Bird his good idea. She said it was a very good one.

Hippo said **sorry** to everyone.

He said **sorry** to Mrs. Croc.

He said **sorry** to Hattie the cat, too!

Then Hippo asked Mrs. Croc if she would help him bake a new chocolate cake for everyone. Mrs. Croc gave him **lots of help**. Hippo baked a very good cake. It had lots of chocolate icing on the top, too.

Soon the cake was ready to eat. Everyone went to get a closer look. It looked **delicious**. It smelled **delicious**. Everyone took a bit of cake. It tasted **wonderful**! Hippo was pleased.

Hippo said he was glad he had **owned up** and **made things right**. Then Mrs. Croc asked him if he would like some cake.

Hippo said he did not want any. He said he did not want any chocolate cake **ever again**! Everyone laughed.

27

Note About Sharing This Book

The *Behavior Matters* series has been developed to provide a starting point for further discussion on children's behavior both in relation to themselves and others. The series is set in the jungle with animal characters reflecting typical behavior traits often seen in young children.

Hippo Owns Up

This story explores the problems that arise when we do something wrong, but then do not own up to it. It looks at the consequences of our actions on others. The book also aims to encourage the children to develop strategies in controlling their behavior and examines ways to make things right when they do something wrong.

How to use the book

The book is designed for adults to share with either an individual child, or a group of children, and as a starting point for discussion.

The book also provides visual support and repeated words and phrases to build reading confidence.

Before reading the story

Choose a time to read when you and the children are relaxed and have time to share the story.

Spend time looking at the illustrations and talk about what the book might be about before reading it together.

Encourage children to employ a phonics first approach to tackling new words by sounding the words out.

After reading, talk about the book with the children:

- Talk about the story with the children. Encourage them to retell the events in chronological order.

- Ask them to express their opinions about Hippo's behavior. Do they think he was wrong to let Hattie, the cat, take the blame? Should he have owned up sooner?

- Invite the children to relate their own experiences of owning up about something they have done wrong in the past to the others. How did they feel before they owned up? How did they feel afterwards? What consequences did their actions have on other people? Did someone else get blamed instead? How did they feel about this? How did they make things right?

- Talk about the importance of saying "sorry" to the people who have been upset by their actions. Remind them that this can also make the person feel better.

- Place children into groups of three or four. Invite them to make up a short play about someone doing something wrong, blaming others and the consequences that follow. Remind the children that each little play should demonstrate how the perpetrator made things right.

- Invite the groups in turn to show their plays to the others. Encourage the others to comment on them and to rate the effectiveness of how things were made right.

29

GLOSSARY

brave having or showing courage

disturb to interrupt or get in the way

late doing something after the time it was supposed to be done

make things right to fix a problem you caused

own up to say you made a mistake or did something bad

worried having thought about something too much, especially something that might be bad

FOR MORE INFORMATION

Berger, Samantha. *Martha Doesn't Say Sorry*. New York: Little, Brown Books for Young Readers, 2011.

Mulcahy, William. *Zach Apologizes*. Minneapolis, MN: Free Spirit Publishing, 2012.

Parr, Todd. *It's Okay to Make Mistakes*. New York: Little, Brown Books for Young Readers, 2014.

INDEX